THE PEOPLE OF THE BOOK

Quran Stories for Little Hearts

by

S A N I Y A S N A I N   K H A N

Goodword**kidz**

Helping you build a family of faith

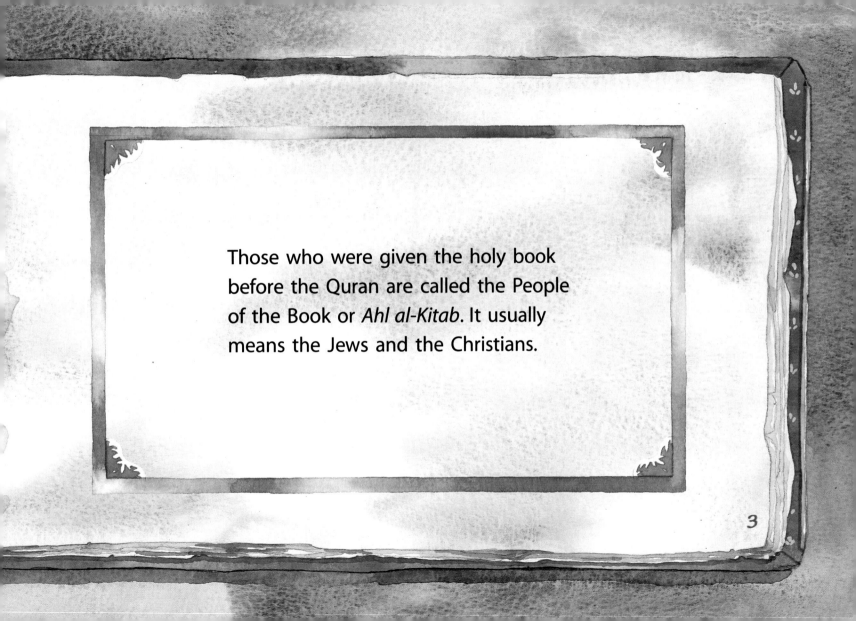

Those who were given the holy book before the Quran are called the People of the Book or *Ahl al-Kitab*. It usually means the Jews and the Christians.

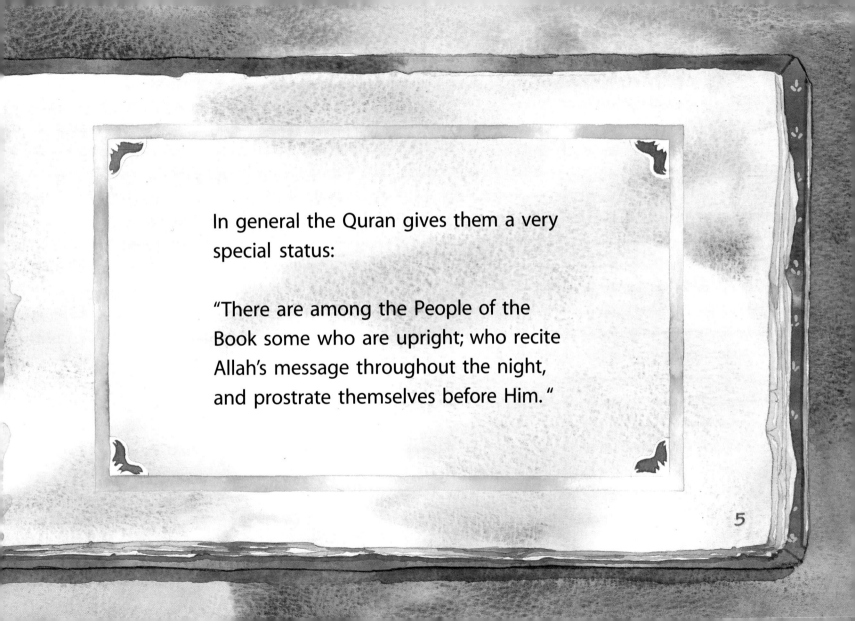

In general the Quran gives them a very special status:

"There are among the People of the Book some who are upright; who recite Allah's message throughout the night, and prostrate themselves before Him. "

The Quran goes on to say about them:

"They believe in Allah and the Last Day, and enjoin the doing of what is right and forbid the doing of what is wrong and compete with one another in doing good works."

Muslims are asked to argue with them in "the most courteous manner:"

"Say: 'We believe in that which is revealed to us and which was revealed to you. Our God and your God is one. To Him we surrender ourselves."

10

The Quran further encourages talk of beliefs held by Jews, Christians and Muslims alike:

"Say: People of the Book! Come to that belief which we and you hold in common: that we will worship only God, that we will treat none as His equal, and that none of us shall take human beings as gods besides Him."

Among the other People of the Book, the Quran considers the Christians as the nearest in brotherly love to the Muslims:

"The nearest of them in affection to the believers are those who say: 'We are Christians.' That is because there are priests and monks among them, and because they are free from pride."

14

The Quran also mentions many
prophets who came to the earth
from time to time to teach the
divine message to people. Some
of the prophets are those who are
held in deep respect by the
People of the Book.

16

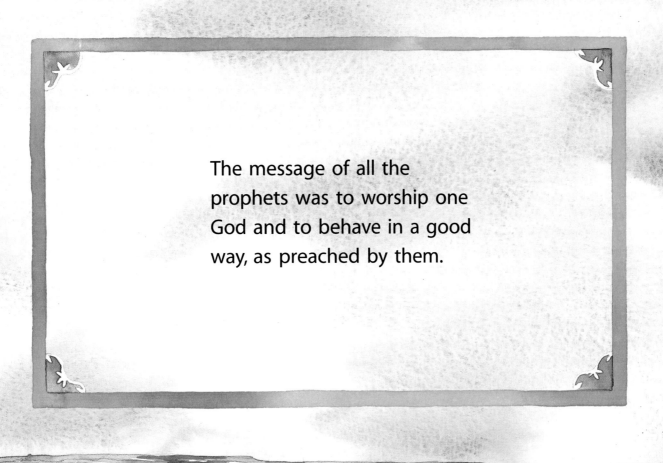

The message of all the prophets was to worship one God and to behave in a good way, as preached by them.

The Quran mentions twenty-five major prophets whose Arabic names and English equivalents are given here:

1. Adam (Adam) علیهِ السلام
2. Idris (Enoch) علیهِ السلام
3. Nuh (Noah) علیهِ السلام
4. Hud علیهِ السلام

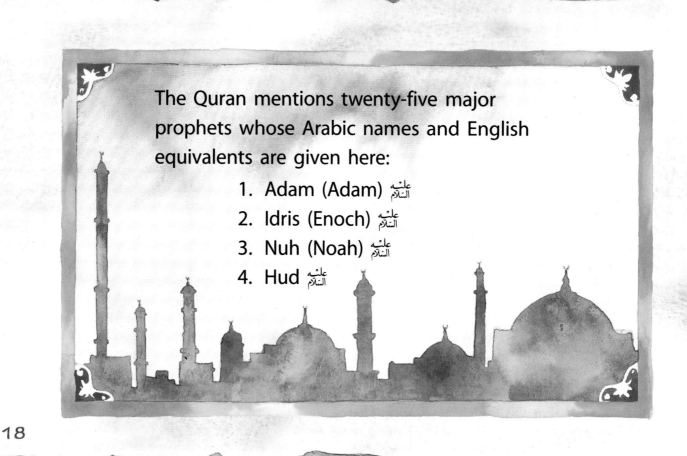

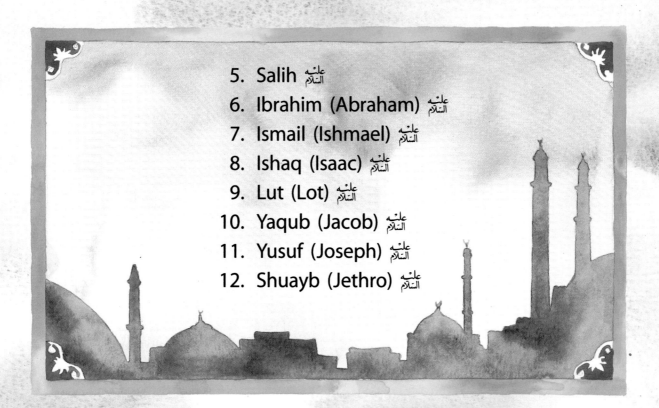

5. Salih عليه السلام

6. Ibrahim (Abraham) عليه السلام

7. Ismail (Ishmael) عليه السلام

8. Ishaq (Isaac) عليه السلام

9. Lut (Lot) عليه السلام

10. Yaqub (Jacob) عليه السلام

11. Yusuf (Joseph) عليه السلام

12. Shuayb (Jethro) عليه السلام

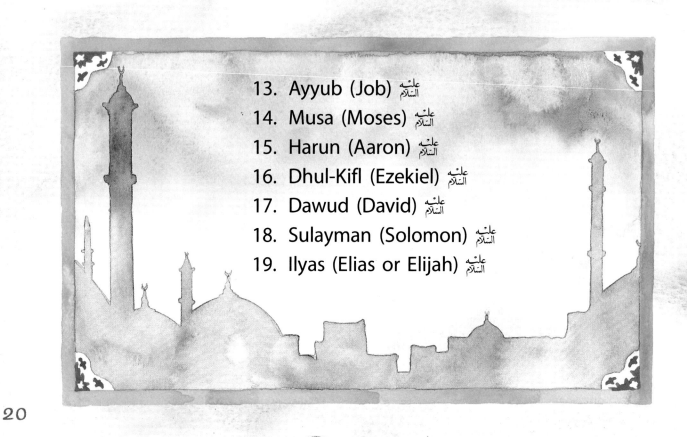

13. Ayyub (Job) عليه السلام

14. Musa (Moses) عليه السلام

15. Harun (Aaron) عليه السلام

16. Dhul-Kifl (Ezekiel) عليه السلام

17. Dawud (David) عليه السلام

18. Sulayman (Solomon) عليه السلام

19. Ilyas (Elias or Elijah) عليه السلام

20. Alyasa (Elisha) عَلَيْهِ السَّلَام
21. Yunus (Jonah) عَلَيْهِ السَّلَام
22. Zakariyya (Zachariah) عَلَيْهِ السَّلَام
23. Yahya (John) عَلَيْهِ السَّلَام
24. Isa (Jesus) عَلَيْهِ السَّلَام
25. Muhammad ﷺ

Some of these prophets were given divine Books (*kutub*) and some were given Scriptures (*suhuf*). The book revealed to the Prophet Musa (Moses) عليه السلام was known as *Tawrat* (the Torah) and the book revealed to the Prophet Isa (Jesus) عليه السلام was known as *Injil* or the Gospel of Jesus.

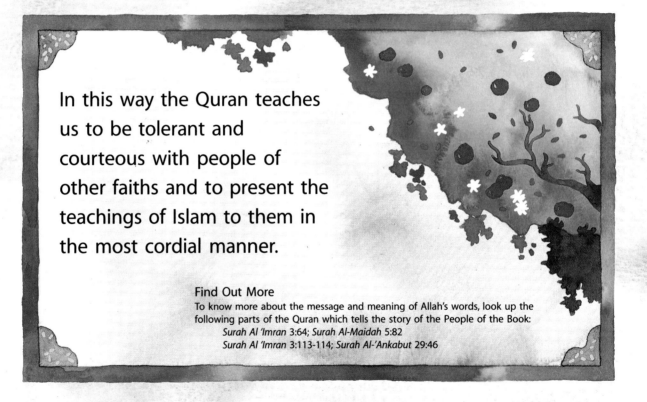

In this way the Quran teaches us to be tolerant and courteous with people of other faiths and to present the teachings of Islam to them in the most cordial manner.

Find Out More
To know more about the message and meaning of Allah's words, look up the following parts of the Quran which tells the story of the People of the Book:
Surah Al 'Imran 3:64; Surah Al-Maidah 5:82
Surah Al 'Imran 3:113-114; Surah Al-'Ankabut 29:46